GW00858704

Please return this book on or before the date shown above. To renew go to www.essex.gov.uk/libraries, ring 0345 603 7628 or go to any Essex library.

Essex County Council

Physical literacy consultants: Dr. Lowri Cerys Edwards and Dr. Lucy Jane Griffiths

LADYBIRD BOOKS

UK | USA | Canada | Ireland | Australia
India | New Zealand | South Africa

Ladybird Books is part of the Penguin Random House group of companies
whose addresses can be found at global.penguinrandomhouse.com.
www.penguin.co.uk   www.puffin.co.uk   www.ladybird.co.uk

Penguin
Random House
UK

First published 2021
001

Printed in China

A CIP catalogue record for this book is available from the British Library

ISBN: 978–0–241–39058–0

All correspondence to:
Ladybird Books
Penguin Random House Children's
One Embassy Gardens, 8 Viaduct Gardens, London SW11 7BW

MIX
Paper from
responsible sources
FSC
www.fsc.org   FSC® C018179

Tips for grown-ups

Name: High Dwight

Letter sound: **igh** as in 'h**igh**'

Favourite activity: high jump

Action: Reach your arms to the sky and try to balance on your toes.

Actiphons is an energetic phonics programme designed for young learners.

Each of the 70 collectable stories stars its own playful character and practises their letter sound and action. By reading the stories in order, children will build their phonics skills and become active, lifelong readers.

How to help your child to read

- Read the words in small type and encourage your child to read the words in big type. Remind them to sound out and then blend together the sounds in each word to read it. For example, "**j-o-g**, jog", "**s-ai-l**, sail" or "**qu-i-ck-er**, quicker".

- If your child struggles with a word, help them to sound it out. If they still find it difficult, just read the word to them and move on.

- You can use the activities at the back of this book for extra practice. Have fun!

High Dwight is very tall.

He has a long, thin neck.

Dwight is good at finding things.

He can see things that are high up.

Cricket Craig has lost his cap.

My cap is up high.

Dwight can help Craig.

I might get it! can go up high.

Dwight is always very helpful.

Yes! Dwight got my cap. He is fab.

He is always very kind, too.

Dwight got my big red bag.

Dwight is going for a walk in the forest.

This is fab.
All the bugs
are up high.

Incredible Isabelle cannot find her cat.

Can you see my cat, Dwight? Is he up high?

The sun is setting. It is hard to see where Isabelle's cat has gone.

Sigh! The light is dim!

The cat is stuck in the tree!

I can see the cat. He is up high, but he is not sad.

Dwight reaches up.

I might! He is high.

Can you get him?

14

He tries again.

Right. I will get on the tips of my feet!

Dwight gets the cat down . . . just in time for bed!

Isabelle is very happy that her cat is safe.

You are back!
You will not
be in the tree
all night.

Your turn!

Can you go up on your tiptoes like High Dwight?

Reach your arms to the sky and try to balance on your toes.

To see a video of this action, listen to the story or sing the song, go to **www.ladybirdeducation.co.uk**. Click **'Unlock book'** and enter this code:

ZW9SY18EWs

What next?

Talk about it

- What did High Dwight do to help Incredible Isabelle?

- Do you think it would be fun to have a very long neck, like Dwight? What would be good about it?

Phonics fun

- Can your child find the **igh** sound in Dwight's name? Emphasize the sound as you say the name.

- Give your child the book. How many words with **igh** in them can your child find in 30 seconds?

Get active!

- Draw a line in chalk outside, or put down a scarf or a piece of string in a straight line indoors. Ask your child to walk slowly along the line on their tiptoes without wobbling. Challenge them to stand on the line and reach up as high as they can. How long can they balance on their toes?

Turn the page to find your next Actiphons story!

Collect Actiphons Level 2